THE ADVENTURES OF
MAN SPONGE
AND BOY PATRICK

IN GOODNESS, MAN RAY!

BY DAVID LEWMAN | ILLUSTRATED BY THE ARTIFACT GROUP

SIMON AND SCHUSTER/NICKELODEON

Based on the TV series *SpongeBob SquarePants*™ created by Stephen Hillenburg as seen on Nickelodeon™

SIMON AND SCHUSTER
First published in Great Britain in 2012 by Simon & Schuster UK Ltd
1st Floor, 222 Gray's Inn Road, London WC1X 8HB
A CBS Company

Originally published in the USA in 2011 by Simon Spotlight, an imprint of Simon & Schuster Children's Division, New York.
© 2012 Viacom International Inc. All rights reserved.
NICKELODEON, SpongeBob SquarePants, and all related titles, logos and characters are trademarks of Viacom International Inc.
Created by Stephen Hillenburg.

A CIP catalogue record for this book is available from the British Library

ISBN   978-0-85707-336-5

Printed and bound by CPI Group (UK) Ltd, Croydon, CR0 4YY

1 3 5 7 9 10 8 6 4 2

Designed by Victor Joseph Ochoa

TABLE OF CONTENTS

DUTY CALLS.....................1

GREAT WALL OF GADGETS......8

OH, TARTAR SAUCE!...........19

FREE TO LAUGH...............30

GOODNESS LESSON #1........38

GOODNESS LESSON #2.......48

GOODNESS LESSON #3........54

GRADUATION DAY............60

THE SMELL OF DEFEAT.........67

TO THE RESCUE!...............72

GIVE ME YOUR HA HA HAS...81

GOODNESS RULES............89

DUTY CALLS

SpongeBob pounded on Patrick's rock. "Patrick! Come on! It's time!"

His buddy's house flipped open with Patrick attached. He looked sleepy. "Time for what?" he mumbled. "A nap?"

"No!" SpongeBob said, shaking his head. "Time for us to visit . . . THE MERMALAIR!"

Patrick looked excited. "Oh yeah!" He hopped down and slammed his house shut. "I remember everything now! Except for two things: What's the Mermalair and why are we going there?"

As they hurried along the sidewalk together, SpongeBob reminded Patrick that the Mermalair was the supersecret headquarters of Bikini Bottom's boldest (and oldest) superheroes: Mermaidman and his faithful sidekick, Barnacleboy!

"They're going on holiday to Leisure Village," SpongeBob explained. "And while they're gone, you and I get to take care of the Mermalair!"

Patrick stopped in his tracks. "That sounds like an awfully big job," he said. "Too big for you and me."

SpongeBob nodded. "You might be right, Patrick." He rubbed his chin, thinking hard. Then he snapped his fingers. "But it's not too big of a job for . . .

MAN SPONGE AND BOY PATRICK!

"Who are they?" asked Patrick, puzzled. "Are you sure they're available?"

SpongeBob chuckled. "Yes, I'm sure," he said. Then he lowered his voice to a whisper. "Because Man Sponge and Boy Patrick are you and me!"

"Oh boy!" Patrick said, grinning. "Which one am I?"

As SpongeBob explained who was who, the two best friends rushed out to the edge of Bikini Bottom. Eventually they arrived at a rock wall. It looked smooth, but if you examined it closely,

you could see the outline of a door cleverly hidden in the stone.

"This is it!" SpongeBob cried. "The secret entrance to the secret Mermalair, where Mermaidman and Barnacleboy secretly keep all their hidden secrets!"

Patrick stared at the rock wall. "How do we get in?"

SpongeBob looked around to see if anyone was listening. When he was sure the coast

was clear, he put his hand up to his mouth and whispered, "Well, Boy Patrick, the secret to getting inside the Mermalair was personally entrusted to me, Man Sponge, by none other than Mermaidman himself!"

"Wow!" Patrick said, impressed.

"The secret is," SpongeBob continued, "we ring the doorbell."

"Brilliant, Man Sponge!"

SpongeBob rang the doorbell.

BING BONG!

They waited impatiently. Inside, the two aging superheroes made their way to the entrance. When the rock door slid open, SpongeBob and Patrick leaped inside, saluting.

"Man Sponge . . . ," SpongeBob shouted.

"And Boy Patrick . . . ," Patrick added.

"REPORTING FOR DUTY!" they yelled together.

"Yeah, yeah," Barnacleboy said, closing the door behind them. "Follow me."

GREAT WALL OF GADGETS

Barnacleboy led SpongeBob and Patrick deeper into the shadowy cave. Mermaidman, who'd fallen asleep standing by the front door, suddenly awoke and cried out,

"EEEEVVVILLLLL!!!"

As they walked past dripping stalactites and lumpy stalagmites, SpongeBob saw strange, glowing computers and bizarre crime-fighting contraptions. He was so excited, he could barely bring himself to concentrate on what Barnacleboy was saying.

"Now, we want you boys to keep an *eye* on the place," Barnacleboy explained. "Water the plants and make sure—"

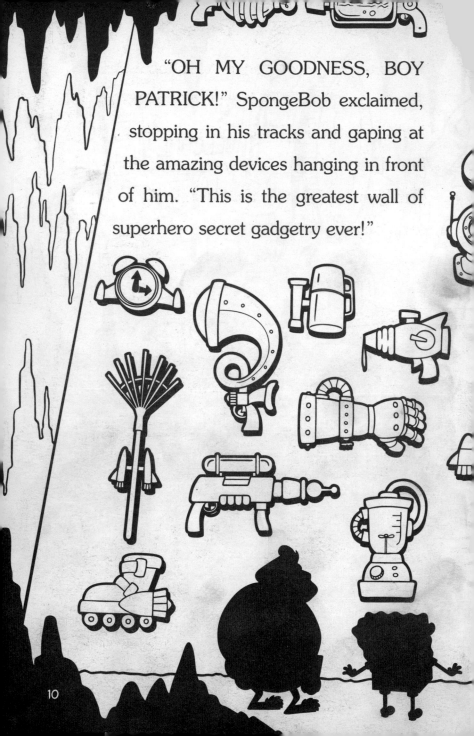

"OH MY GOODNESS, BOY PATRICK!" SpongeBob exclaimed, stopping in his tracks and gaping at the amazing devices hanging in front of him. "This is the greatest wall of superhero secret gadgetry ever!"

It was a wall covered in weird tools and appliances. SpongeBob couldn't wait to get his hands on the astonishing objects he'd heard about in Mermaidman's adventures. "I'm gonna play with the Cosmic Ray!" he sang out.

"I get the Aqua Glove!" Patrick called.

They rushed toward the wall of gadgets, but Mermaidman leaped in front of them, blocking the way. "Hold on there, boys!" he cried. "You cannot play with this stuff!"

SpongeBob backed off, but turned toward a white ball on top of a brass pole. "What about the Orb of Confusion?" he asked, flipping its switch from off to on.

Odd waves passed through the air, like ripples spreading from a rock thrown in water. SpongeBob immediately felt very confused. He stuck out his tongue and rolled his eyes. "DOY! DOYEEE! DUUHHHH!"

Mermaidman quickly turned off the orb. "No!" he gasped. "Prolonged exposure to the Orb of Confusion will give you, uh, confusion!"

SpongeBob snapped out of his state of confusion and grinned. "Of course!" he said. "I remember the Orb of Confusion from one of your greatest adventures, when you captured Man Ray!"

"How did that one go?" asked Mermaidman, scratching his head.

Patrick spoke up. "Man Ray was a bad guy and you wanted to stop the bad guys, so you stopped him!" Patrick was proud of his splendid re-telling of the story.

"Doesn't ring a bell," murmured Mermaidman.

SpongeBob pointed to the Orb of Confusion but didn't touch it this time. "You put the Orb of Confusion right outside the vault in the First Nautical Bank. Then you tricked Man Ray into thinking he had to flip the orb's switch to get into the vault and steal all the money."

Patrick interrupted. "Were Man Sponge
and Boy Patrick there to help?"

"Of course!" SpongeBob answered. "They
helped lure Man Ray into the trap!"

Barnacleboy shook his head. "I don't remember that part."

"Then what happened in the story, Mummy?" Mermaidman asked, a little confused.

"With the help of Man Sponge and Boy Patrick, you captured the evil Man Ray!" SpongeBob said. Patrick clapped his hands. "Good story! Again! Again!"

Barnacleboy picked up his suitcase and headed for the door. "We don't have time for any more stories. Remember, don't touch anything! Especially the Invisible Boatmobile!"

Mermaidman followed his sidekick. "Up, up, and away!" He waddled out of the Mermalair, carrying his luggage.

SpongeBob turned to Patrick, vibrating with excitement. "Just think, Boy Patrick!" he said. "Now WE'RE in charge!"

OH, TARTAR SAUCE!

SpongeBob struck a manly pose. "Come, Boy Patrick! While our heroes are away, we will keep evil at bay!"

He jumped deeper into the cave, flipping and making karate sounds.

20

Patrick followed, kicking the air with his pink legs.

But as he turned a corner in the cave, Patrick spotted something that made him freeze in his tracks. Trembling, he tried to tell SpongeBob what he saw. "M-m-m-m-m . . ."

SpongeBob heard Patrick and came back to where he stood, shaking with fear. "What is it, trusted sidekick?" he asked.

Patrick still couldn't get out the words. "M-m-m-m . . ."

SpongeBob peered into a cavernous chamber and saw what had frightened Patrick. Shuddering, he couldn't get out the words either. "M-m-m-m . . ."

They clung to each other, terrified. Finally they managed to force out the words they'd been trying to say to each other.

"MAN RAY!!!"

The evil supervillain stood in a dark room, stretching his gloved hands toward SpongeBob and Patrick.

"AAAHH!!"

they screamed, dashing away.

SpongeBob realized Man Ray wasn't chasing them. He tiptoed back to meet Patrick. "How come he's not chasing us, Man Sponge?" Patrick asked.

Man Sponge decided he needed to investigate further. He took a deep breath to calm himself and crept toward Man Ray. The villain stood absolutely still, not making a sound.

"Looks like he's frozen or something, Boy Patrick."

Patrick shivered, muttering, "Fro-fro-fro-fro-fro-fro . . ."

Man Sponge fearlessly approached Man Ray, until he could see that the villain was inside a column of cold, white goo. Knocking on the column, he said, "It appears to be some sort of prison chamber . . ."—he licked the goo—"made out of frozen tartar sauce!"

SpongeBob stood back admiring the tartar-sauce trap. "This is incredible! Next to the Dirty Bubble, the evil Man Ray is the all-time greatest arch-nemesis of Mermaidman and Barnacleboy. I have so many questions to ask him!"

At that very moment, the tartar sauce holding Man Ray started to melt. Laughing goofily, Patrick stood by a control switch he had flipped from FREEZE to UNFREEZE.

SpongeBob ran over to Patrick. "Pat, what are you doing? We're not supposed to touch anything!"

Patrick looked puzzled. "But you said you had a question."

"We could get in trouble!" SpongeBob cried.

"That's not a question," answered Patrick.

While they argued, the tartar sauce melted down past Man Ray's head. His eyes glowed a menacing red.

"They said not to touch anything and that includes unfreezing a supervillain," SpongeBob insisted.

Then, from above their heads, came a low, evil voice. "I'm FREE!" it gloated, laughing a horrible laugh!

FREE TO LAUGH

"Actually, Mr. Man Ray, sir," SpongeBob pointed out, "only your head is free." The white goo had only melted down to Man Ray's shoulders.

Man Ray looked down and saw that it was true. He was still trapped. "By the supreme authority of wickedness," he growled, "I, the evil Man Ray, command you to release me from this frozen prison at once!"

SpongeBob twiddled his fingers nervously. "Well, Mr. Evil Man Ray, sir, we can't do that."

"WHY NOT?" Man Ray roared. The force

of his powerful voice blew SpongeBob and Patrick back on their heels.

SpongeBob frowned and pointed at Man Ray accusingly. "Because you're EVIL!"

Man Ray thought a moment. Then he spoke, more gently this time. "You mean if I was *good* you'd let me go?"

"Yeah, sure. Why not?" SpongeBob said, shrugging his shoulders. Patrick nodded.

Man Ray saw his chance for escape. "In that case," he said in as friendly a voice as he could manage, "I *am* good!"

SpongeBob's eyes opened wide. "Really?"

Man Ray nodded. "Yes, really."

"Really really?" SpongeBob asked.

"Yes, really really," Man Ray answered, slightly annoyed.

"Really really really?" SpongeBob asked.

"YES, YES ALREADY! I'M GOOD! I'M GOOD!" Man Ray shouted. "Now let me out of here or you'll suffer dire consequences!"

SpongeBob turned to Patrick and shrugged. "Well, that's good enough for me!" He grabbed the big switch and pulled it all the way down from FREEZE to UNFREEZE.

The white goo thawed quickly, starting at the top, around Man Ray's shoulders, and melting down past his feet until he was completely free. He fell to his knees on the ground and looked up with an evil glint in his eyes.

"You fools!" he sneered. "Prepare to be eradicated!"

Man Ray leaped toward SpongeBob and Patrick, but in midair he grabbed his stomach and started to laugh. He fell to the ground, laughing helplessly and clutching his stomach. Smiling, SpongeBob walked up to him with a remote control in his hand.

The belt around Man Ray's waist was vibrating, tickling him mercilessly. "What is this infernal contraption?" he managed to gasp between laughs.

Looking sly, SpongeBob pointed toward the helpless Man Ray. "Don't play dumb, Man Ray! You know that's the Tickle Belt that Mermaidman used on you in Episode Seventeen!"

"Oh, I LOVE that episode!" Patrick said.

Man Ray kept laughing as the belt kept tickling him.

"Remember how Mermaidman tricked Man Ray into putting on the belt by telling him it would match his costume perfectly?" SpongeBob asked.

"Oh yeah!" Patrick said. "But didn't Mermaidman get a lot of help from Man Sponge and Boy Patrick?"

"I think you're right, Patrick!" SpongeBob said, grinning.

"That's not the way I remember it," Man Ray said, still giggling and guffawing.

While SpongeBob and Patrick chattered away about their adventures as Man Sponge and Boy Patrick, Man Ray thought to himself, *I need an evil plan that will trick them into taking this belt off me. Time for those acting lessons to pay off!*

GOODNESS LESSON #1

"Oh, boo-hoo! Oh, sob! Oh, cry!" Man Ray wailed.

SpongeBob and Patrick stopped talking and looked at Man Ray, puzzled. Why was he crying?

"Oh, woe is me! You don't know what it's like, being evil for so long!" Man Ray raised his fist in the air dramatically. "Oh, how I wish to be good! If only some kind heroes would show me the path to decency!"

SpongeBob gasped with excitement and turned toward Patrick. "Did you hear that? 'Kind heroes'!"

Patrick nodded. "This is a job for . . ."

MAN SPONGE AND BOY PATRICK!

The two friends bumped their fists together and approached Man Ray, who was still pretending to weep. SpongeBob cleared his throat to get his attention. "Um, Mr. Man Ray? We could teach you how to be good! And then we'll let you go!"

Man Ray stood up and looked grateful. "Ah, that would be fantastic!" he said. Then he turned away and spoke quietly to himself. "I'll fake my way through this just like I did in high school." He chuckled and rubbed his hands together gleefully.

SpongeBob and Patrick found a school desk in the depths of the Mermalair and invited Man Ray to sit in it. He sat down and politely folded his hands on top of the desk.

"Okay, Man Ray," SpongeBob said. "Are you ready for your first day at Goodness School?"

Man Ray quickly placed an apple on top of the desk. SpongeBob was impressed. *What a nice gift for a pupil to give his teacher!*

SpongeBob elbowed his sidekick. "Pat, get your wallet out." He turned back to Man Ray. "Okay, Goodness Lesson Number One: You see someone drop their wallet."

Patrick just stood there holding his wallet. SpongeBob whispered, "Patrick, drop the wallet." He dropped his wallet on the cave floor.

SpongeBob addressed Man Ray. "Now what would you do?"

Man Ray got up from his desk, picked up the wallet, and politely offered it to Patrick. "Excuse me, sir, but I do believe you've dropped your wallet."

Patrick just stared at the wallet. "It doesn't look familiar to me."

This answer took Man Ray by surprise. "What? I just saw you drop it." He offered the wallet again. "Here."

Patrick didn't take it. "Nope. It's not mine."

Man Ray tried to stay patient. "It is yours. I am trying to be a good person and return it to you."

"Return what to who?" Patrick said dully.

Man Ray slapped his hand to his face in frustration. Then he got an idea. He opened the wallet and found Patrick's ID card. "Aren't you Patrick Star?"

"Yup," Patrick said, nodding.

Man Ray showed the ID card to Patrick. "And this is your ID?"

"Yup," Patrick said.

Man Ray smiled. This was going well. "I found this ID in this wallet. And if that's the case, this must be your wallet!"

Patrick agreed. "That makes sense to me."

Man Ray put the ID back in the wallet and offered it to Patrick. "Then take it!"

"It's not my wallet," Patrick said.

Bikini Bottom
Card of Identification
(This is not a driver's license!)

4-8-15-16-23-42

Patrick Star
120 Conch St. Bikini Bottom
V5311988

PATRICK
STAR

Furious, Man Ray crushed the wallet in his hand and raised it above his head threateningly. "You dim bulb! Take back your wallet or I'll rip your arms off!" he roared.

Suddenly the Tickle Belt vibrated. Man Ray clutched his stomach and bent over, laughing.

"Wrong!" SpongeBob said sternly as he pushed the button on the belt's remote control.

"Good people don't rip other people's arms off!"

GOODNESS LESSON #2

SpongeBob stood ready to press the Tickle Belt button again if Man Ray turned violent. "Okay, Goodness Lesson Number Two," he said.

Patrick entered the cave room carrying a cardboard box. SpongeBob gestured toward him, asking Man Ray, "You see someone struggling with a heavy package. What do you do?"

As Patrick walked forward, huffing and puffing, Man Ray said, "Hello, friend! I noticed you were struggling with that package. Would you like some help with—"

WHAAM!!

Patrick accidentally dropped the heavy box on Man Ray's foot. "OW!" Man Ray yelled.

"Oops," Patrick said. "Sorry. Can I start over?"

He picked up the box. Man Ray reached for it, saying, "I noticed you were

SLAAM!!

Patrick accidentally dropped the box on Man Ray's foot again! "OWWW!" Man Ray howled.

"Oops! Gotta start again," Patrick said, picking up the box.

"Would you—YAAAAAHHH!" Man Ray wailed. Patrick had dropped the box on his foot for the third time. "Oops," he said.

Man Ray pointed at Patrick, shaking with anger. "You butter-fingered pink thing! What's in that box, anyhow?"

"My wallets," Patrick answered.

"YAARRGGHHH!" Man Ray yelled. He grabbed the top of Patrick's head and lifted him off the ground.

"SpongeBob! Tickle him!" Patrick cried.

Man Ray slammed Patrick onto the cave floor. Then he lifted him up and did it again. And again!

SpongeBob punched the button, turning on the Tickle Belt. Man Ray started laughing but kept throwing Patrick around.

"It tickles!" Man Ray gasped between laughs. "But it's worth it!"

GOODNESS LESSON #3

SpongeBob stood holding the remote control. "All right, Goodness Lesson Number Three." He put his finger to his chin, thinking. "Uh, let's see . . ."

Patrick snatched the control from SpongeBob. He was wearing bandages and sitting in a wheelchair.

"I've got one," he said, scowling at Man Ray. "I'm

thinking of a number between one and one hundred. What is it?"

Man Ray looked confused. He scratched his head. "Um . . . sixty-two?"

"Wrong!" Patrick cried, punching the button on the remote control.

The belt started vibrating, tickling Man Ray. "HEE HEE HEE! STOP! STOP! HA HA HA!"

But Patrick kept pressing the button, tickling Man Ray more and more. SpongeBob looked concerned. "Hey, Patrick," he said. "That's got nothing to do with being good." He grabbed the remote control and tried to yank it away from Patrick.

"Let go of it, SpongeBob," Patrick snarled, still mad at Man Ray for hurting him.

"Pat, we've got to use it only when he's bad!" SpongeBob argued.

"Let go!" Patrick insisted.

"No, *you* let go!" SpongeBob said.

While they wrestled over the remote control, Man Ray was helplessly rolling on the floor, laughing and giggling.

"This is NOT the Man Sponge and Boy Patrick way!" SpongeBob yelled.

"Maybe not," Patrick said. "But it's the Patrick way!"

"LET . . . GO!" SpongeBob and Patrick said at the same time.

Then . . .

SNAP!

The remote control pulled apart, flew out of their hands, and broke into a thousand pieces. The belt started to tickle Man Ray even more deeply, and there was nothing SpongeBob could do to stop it!

"HA HA HA HA!" Man Ray laughed. "Frequency rising . . . belt out of control . . . belt on too high . . . tickling my DNA!"

Man Ray laughed until tears came out of his eyes. "Make it stop! PLEASE!"

SpongeBob and Patrick looked at each other, surprised.

GRADUATION DAY

As Man Ray kept laughing
helplessly, SpongeBob
turned to Patrick. "Did
you hear that, Patrick?"

"Man Ray laughing?"
Patrick asked. "I sure did. I wonder
what's so funny."

SpongeBob shook his head. "No, I mean
he said the *P*-word!"

"Peanuts?" Patrick guessed.

"Nope," SpongeBob said.

"Patrick?"

"Nope. Man Ray said 'please'!"

Patrick realized SpongeBob was right. He *had* said "please"!

"Well," Patrick said, shrugging, "that's good enough for me. I guess he's reconstituted."

"Rehabilitated," SpongeBob whispered to his friend, gently correcting him.

"Gesundheit," Patrick said.

SpongeBob pulled a big brass key out of his pocket and held it up in the air triumphantly. "It's Graduation Day, Man Ray!" he announced. "This is the key to your future!"

Man Ray was still writhing on the floor, laughing uncontrollably. SpongeBob started to walk over to him, but Patrick grabbed his arm, stopping him.

"Wait a minute, SpongeBob," he said. "Are you sure this is right?"

"What do you mean?" SpongeBob asked. "You said yourself he was reconstituted—I mean rehabilitated."

"I mean, if this is his Graduation Day, shouldn't there be music? And a diploma? And a guest speaker?" Patrick asked.

SpongeBob frowned, thinking. "We don't really have time for all that, Patrick. Besides, who would be the guest speaker?"

"Um, Man Sponge?" Patrick suggested. "Ooh! Ooh! Or, I know, Boy Patrick!"

Man Ray continued to squirm on the floor. His stomach was getting really sore from all the laughing.

"Well, Boy Patrick," SpongeBob said, "if you want to, feel free to provide the music."

"You got it, Man Sponge!" Patrick said. He started to sing a solemn song with no words. "Bum bum-bum-bum bum-bum, bum bum-bum-bum bum-bum . . ."

In time to the music SpongeBob marched over to Man Ray. He put the key in the belt's lock and turned it. The belt sprang open and stopped vibrating. Man Ray stopped laughing.

Then Man Ray smiled . . . an evil, devious smile. He leaped to his feet and raised both arms in triumph.

"Just look at him, Patrick," SpongeBob said happily. "The picture of goodness!"

Patrick put his arm around SpongeBob's shoulders, pleased with their excellent teaching.

Then Man Ray dashed over to the wall of superhero secret gadgetry!

THE SMELL OF DEFEAT

Chuckling with evil delight, Man Ray pulled a dangerous-looking gadget from the wall. It was a shiny metal glove that went all the way up to the wearer's elbow.

SpongeBob raised a finger to get Man Ray's attention. "Um, we're not supposed to touch that stuff."

But Man Ray just ignored SpongeBob, slipping the glove onto his left arm. With his right arm he clicked on the glove, getting it ready for action.

SpongeBob looked worried. "We're not supposed to touch that either."

Man Ray turned back to the wall again and reached for something that looked like an explosive hand grenade. Sniggering, he attached it to the metal glove.

"We're *really* not supposed to touch those, sir," SpongeBob pleaded, putting his hands up as if to say *stop*.

Laughing cruelly, Man Ray raised the index finger on the metal glove and aimed it right at SpongeBob and Patrick!

But SpongeBob just went right on lecturing Man Ray. "Good people have no use for weapons such as those . . ."

ZAAAP!

Man Ray fired a blast of energy right at SpongeBob and Patrick! They were lifted off the ground, their skeletons showing through their skin. "YAAAAGGGHHH!" they screamed.

Man Ray pointed his smoking finger in the air and scowled at his two victims. "The only thing I'm good at is being evil!" he snarled.

Then he turned and pressed a button on the wall. The door to the Mermalair slid open. As he ran out into Bikini Bottom, Man Ray called back over his shoulder, "So long, hopeless do-gooders!"

SpongeBob and Patrick were left behind. They were smouldering piles of ash and soot. They were also very disappointed in their Goodness student.

"What's that smell?" Patrick asked.

SpongeBob sighed. "That, Patrick, is the smell of defeat."

"Oh," Patrick said. "I thought it was my skin."

SpongeBob shrugged off his disappointment and raised his smoky chin. "Forget about your skin, Patrick! Man Ray is still bad and someone has to stop him!"

SpongeBob was full of determination. "This is a job for Man Sponge!"

"And Boy Patrick!" Patrick added.

TO THE RESCUE!

SpongeBob and Patrick scooted across the floor toward a pair of ropes that led to a lower level of the Mermalair. They leaped onto the ropes and slid down to the lower level. When they reached the bottom, they were dressed as superheroes! Man Sponge and Boy Patrick, that is!

"How are we going to catch up with Man Ray, Man Sponge?" the faithful sidekick asked. "He's pretty speedy."

"True, Boy Patrick, true." Man Sponge used all the power of his spongy brain. "I know! We'll

borrow the Invisible Boatmobile!"

"But wasn't that one of the things we weren't supposed to touch?" Boy Patrick pointed out.

That was a good point, so Man Sponge again put his brain to work. "Well," he said, "SpongeBob and Patrick weren't supposed to touch the Invisible Boatmobile. But they didn't say anything about Man Sponge and Boy Patrick!"

Boy Patrick brightened. "That is good thinking, SpongeBob!

I mean, Man Sponge!"

"Now all we have to do is find it!"

They started walking around the lower chamber of the Mermalair with their arms stretched out, hoping to feel the Invisible Boatmobile.

"Found it!" Boy Patrick shouted. "But it might need to be fixed. It's squishy and full of holes."

"Boy Patrick, that's not the Boatmobile. That's my head," Man Sponge said.

They kept feeling around until Man Sponge finally found the Invisible Boatmobile.

He climbed into the driver's seat, and Boy Patrick got in next to him.

"IGNITION ON!" Boy Patrick yelled, punching an invisible button on the dashboard. The engine roared.

"WAIT!" Man Sponge cried. "I don't have a licence!"

Boy Patrick thought for a moment. Then he reached into his pocket.

"Well, this is an invisible boat, right?"

"Right . . .," Man Sponge agreed.

"So you need an invisible licence!" Boy Patrick concluded. He held up an invisible licence and handed it to Man Sponge.

"You're the best sidekick ever, Boy Patrick!"

Man Sponge said, accepting the invisible licence gratefully.

Man Sponge grasped the steering wheel and hit the gas. Flames burst out of the back of the Invisible Boatmobile and the boat shot forward.

SMASH!

The heroes crashed through the rock wall of the Mermalair!

"YAAAAAAAAAAAAGGGHHHH!" they screamed.

WHAM!

The Invisible Boatmobile slammed into a light pole. "Thank goodness for invisible seat belts," Boy Patrick said.

Man Ray ran right past them.

"Out of my way, fools!" he sneered. "You no longer have control of me."

He stopped on a rocky outcropping and pointed at Bikini Bottom. "Now this town belongs to Man Ray!"

"Not so fast, arch-villain!" Man Sponge said, climbing out of the boat. "We still have the Orb of Confusion. Take this!"

Man Sponge flipped the switch on the orb. Immediately he and Boy Patrick felt very confused. "Daaaahhh! Doy! Daa heyoooo!" they drooled.

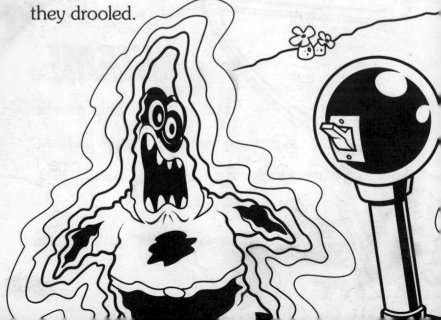

Man Ray shrugged. "Well, that was easy." He left the two heroes babbling and headed straight for the First Nautical Bank!

GIVE ME YOUR HA HA HAS

At the bank several customers stood in line waiting for their turns with the teller. "You know what I like about this bank?" one lady asked another. "It's always so nice and quiet." The other customers nodded in agreement.

Just then . . .

BOOM!

Man Ray kicked open the bank's front door and leaped inside. "All right, people!" he roared. "Everybody stand right where you are!" He pointed the index finger of his metal glove right at the customers, ready to fire.

The customers gasped. It looked as though the bank was being robbed!

Seeing the customers cower, Man Ray smiled to himself. He had them right where he wanted them. Now all he had to do was take their cash and all the money in the bank.

"I want all of you to . . . ," he said, starting to give them instructions.

But suddenly, he felt the strangest urge to laugh!

"I . . . heh heh . . . want you to . . . hee hee hee," he giggled.

Unable to stop himself, Man Ray let out a big laugh. "Ha ha ha!"

The customers were puzzled. What was going on? Was this guy trying to rob the bank or was this some kind of joke?

The teller snickered. The customers started to giggle too.

"No! No!" Man Ray shouted. He was losing control of the situation! "Stop giggling or I'll have to . . . haw haw haw!"

"Ha ha ha!" the customers laughed, thinking the whole thing must be a prank. "Ho ho hee hee hee!"

"STOP LAUGHING, YOU FOOLS!"

Man Ray bellowed. He shoved his way past the customers and went right up to the teller.

"What can I do for you, sir?" she asked politely.

Man Ray pointed his metal glove right in her face. "I'll tell you what you can do!" he

yelled angrily. "Give me all your . . . heh heh heh!"

The teller looked bewildered. "All my what, sir?"

Man Ray struggled to stop laughing. "Give me all your . . . hee hee hee!" He clutched his ribs, hooting and snorting.

"I'm sorry, sir, but I still don't understand what it is that you want me to do," the teller said patiently.

Summoning all his strength, Man Ray tried to stop laughing. "GIVE ME . . . ," he started to say, but it was no use. "HAW HAW HAW HAW HAW!"

He pounded the counter, laughing. He fell to the ground and kicked his heels, rolling around and hugging his sides. He'd never laughed so hard in his life!

Finally he sat up. "The belt is gone," he

said, "but I still feel its tickle!" Then he realized he didn't feel evil anymore. "The urge to do bad is gone," he said, amazed.

Man Ray fell to his knees, defeated. "I guess I'll just open a checking account," he said.

GOODNESS RULES

Back outside the Mermalair, Man Sponge and Boy Patrick were still caught in the befuddling rays coming from the Orb of Confusion.

"DOOOOYYYY!" Man Sponge said with his tongue hanging out of his mouth.

"DUUUUHHHH!" Boy Patrick said with his eyes crossed.

Man Ray calmly walked up and switched off the orb.

"DOYEEEE . . . ," Man Sponge said. Then the confusion left him. He looked up and saw the arch-villain he'd been trying to stop!

"Man Ray!" he gasped.

Man Ray held up a friendly hand in a gesture of peace. "No need to be alarmed, SpongeBob," he said.

"That's Man Sponge," he corrected.

"Whatever," Man Ray said. "Your teachings have transformed me!"

Man Sponge was astonished. "You mean, you aren't evil anymore?"

Man Ray shook his head. "Nope. You tickled the evil right out of me." Then he held up his new checkbook and smiled. "And," he added, "I have checks with little poodles on them!"

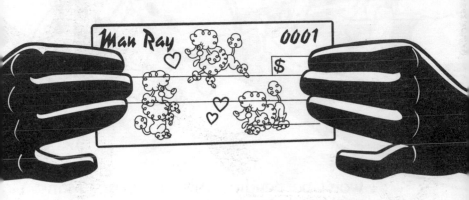

Man Sponge leaned forward to look at the checks. Sure enough, they featured pictures of adorable little poodles!

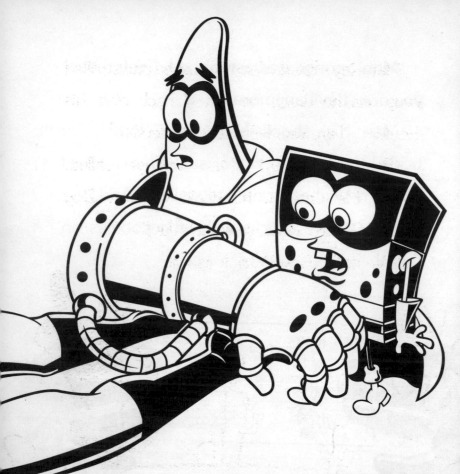

"I won't be needing this anymore," Man Ray said, taking off the metal glove he'd stolen from the Mermalair. He handed it to Man Sponge.

"Thanks," SpongeBob said, staggering a little under the weight of the heavy glove.

Man Ray smiled. Then he turned and strolled away. As he went, he waved back over his shoulder. "Farewell, fellow do-gooders!"

"Bye, Man Ray!" Man Sponge called, waving. He turned to his sidekick. "Wow, Boy Patrick! We did it! We saved the day!"

"We did?" Boy Patrick asked.

"We sure did! We took an evil arch-villain and we turned him good! He'll never bother anyone in Bikini Bottom again!" Man Sponge cheered.

"Wow," Boy Patrick said. "It's like we're superheroes or something."

Man Sponge nodded. "That's because we ARE superheroes! We're Man Sponge . . ."

"And Boy Patrick!"

They pumped their fists and jumped in the air. What a triumph! What an achievement! What an accomplishment!

Mermaidman and Barnacleboy themselves couldn't have done it better.

THE END

SPONGE PATROL!

It was a quiet day in Bikini Bottom, and SpongeBob and Patrick were eager for an adventure.

"I think it's time, Patrick," SpongeBob told his best friend seriously.

"Time for what?" Patrick asked.

"For some superhero action!" SpongeBob cried out.

Five seconds later, Man Sponge and Boy Patrick marched through downtown Bikini Bottom on their daily rounds. The two superheroes were eager to help anyone in trouble.

"Keep a sharp eye out for citizens in need," Man Sponge reminded Boy Patrick.

"Aye, aye, Man Sponge," Boy Patrick answered, saluting.

Suddenly, Man Sponge pointed. "Look, Boy Patrick! A person in distress!"

Boy Patrick peered in the direction Man Sponge was pointing. "You mean that rubbish bin? You're right! It really needs to be emptied!"

"No, I mean the lady next to the rubbish bin!" Man Sponge explained. "She obviously wants to cross the street, but she can't get through the villainous traffic without the aid of . . . MAN SPONGE AND . . ."

"BOY PATRICK!" added Boy Patrick. Together they rushed over to the elderly woman, picked her up, and dashed across the street!

When they reached the opposite side of the busy avenue, they set the lady down. "No need to thank us, ma'am!" Man Sponge said, smiling. "It's all in a day's work for Man Sponge . . ."

"And Boy Patrick!"

The two of them ran off. The woman looked puzzled. "But I didn't *want* to cross the street," she said. "My bus stops on the other side."

By that time, Man Sponge had already moved on to another citizen in need. "Boy Patrick, if I'm not mistaken—and I never am—that young fellow there is being attacked by a vicious creature!"

Without a second's hesitation, the two superheroes sprinted over and got between the beast and the boy. "Run, lad!" shouted

Man Sponge. "We'll handle the monster!"

The boy looked confused. "What monster?"

Boy Patrick pointed at the fearsome beast. "That monster right there!"

The boy looked insulted. "That's not a monster! That's my pet worm, Crawler. I'm taking him for a walk. Come on, boy."

The worm happily followed its owner. Boy Patrick looked concerned. "I don't like this,

Man Sponge. It's like that monster has the kid under some kind of mind-control ray!"

"No time to think about that!" Man Sponge cried. "We've got to save Pearl from the evil Teenage Guy!"

Sure enough, right across the street, Mr. Krabs's daughter, Pearl, was chatting with a teenage boy. "Um, Pearl," he asked nervously, "do you think maybe you might like to go with me to the dance next—"

"HOLD IT RIGHT THERE, TEENAGE GUY!" Man Sponge bellowed. "That fair, young damsel is under the constant protection of Man Sponge . . ."

"And Boy Patrick!" chimed in Boy Patrick.

Pearl looked annoyed. Derek had finally gotten up the nerve to ask her to the dance, and then these two come barging in. "Shouldn't you be at work?" she snapped.

Man Sponge looked at his watch and gasped. "Gadzooks!" he cried. "The lass is right! I'm due at the Krusty Krab, where I toil under the guise of my mild-mannered secret identity, SpongeBob SquarePants!" He dashed off to work.

Derek watched him go. "You know, it's not much of a secret identity if you announce it to everyone," he said.

He and Pearl stood there awkwardly with Patrick for a minute. "So," Patrick asked, "you two want to get a milk shake?"